HEATHCLIFF
SMOOTH SAILING

The funniest feline in America delights millions of fans every day as he appears in over 500 newspapers. You'll have a laugh a minute as Heathcliff tangles with the milkman, the cat show judge, the veterinarian and just about everyone else he runs into. If you're looking for some fun, look no further — Heathcliff is here!

Heathcliff Books

HEATHCLIFF
HEATHCLIFF RIDES AGAIN
HEATHCLIFF TRIPLE THREAT
HEATHCLIFF WANTED
HEATHCLIFF SPINS A YARN
HEATHCLIFF DOES IT AGAIN!
HEATHCLIFF STRIKES AGAIN!
HEATHCLIFF ROUND 3
HEATHCLIFF PIGS OUT
HEATHCLIFF FIRST PRIZE!
HEATHCLIFF'S TREASURE CHEST OF PUZZLES
HEATHCLIFF'S PUZZLERS
HEATHCLIFF PUZZLE SLEUTH
HEATHCLIFF BANQUET
HEATHCLIFF FEAST
SWEET SAVAGE HEATHCLIFF
WICKED LOVING HEATHCLIFF
HEATHCLIFF IN CONCERT
HEATHCLIFF PLAY BY PLAY
HEATHCLIFF DINES OUT
HEATHCLIFF GONE FISHIN'
HEATHCLIFF CLEANS HOUSE
HEATHCLIFF WORKING OUT
HEATHCLIFF CATCH OF THE DAY
HEATHCLIFF ON VACATION
HEATHCLIFF KOOL KAT
HEATHCLIFF ROCKIN' AND ROLLIN'
HEATHCLIFF SMOOTH SAILING

HEATHCLIFF
SMOOTH SAILING

by Geo Gately

JOVE BOOKS, NEW YORK

Cartoons previously published in
Heathcliff In Concert

HEATHCLIFF SMOOTH SAILING

A Jove Book / published by arrangement with
McNaught Syndicate, Inc.

PRINTING HISTORY
Charter Edition / February 1987
Jove edition / April 1987

All rights reserved.
Copyright © 1978, 1979, 1980, 1983, 1985, 1987
by McNaught Syndicate, Inc.
Heathcliff® is a registered trademark of McNaught Syndicate, Inc.
This book may not be reproduced in whole or in part,
by mimeograph or any other means, without permission.
For information address: The Berkley Publishing Group,
200 Madison Avenue, New York, New York 10016.

ISBN: 0-515-09464-1

Jove Books are published by The Berkley Publishing Group,
200 Madison Avenue, New York, New York 10016.
The name "JOVE" and the "J" logo
are trademarks belonging to Jove Publications, Inc.

PRINTED IN THE UNITED STATES OF AMERICA

10   9   8   7   6   5   4   3   2   1

"THE MILK AND COOKIES WILL BE ENOUGH FOR SANTA CLAUS!"

"EEYAH!"

"...OH, IT'S THE JANITOR."

"HIS FRIEND ISN'T AMUSED."

"YOU DID IT!...WHY SHOULD I GET INVOLVED?!"

"COO, COO!... COO, COO!... COO, COO!"

"....AT THIS POINT, THE SAUCER ENCOUNTERED A SMART ALEC...."

"HAH! I GOT HIM GOOD!"

"BUT HE GOT MY DENTURES."

"WILL THE OWNER OF A 1980 RED KITTY SPORT CAR, LICENSE NUMBER 'MEW 123', PLEASE REPORT TO THE PARKING LOT?"

"HE HATES THE MASKED MARVEL!"

"NO WONDER HE WON'T EAT!... THAT'S NOT HIS *THURSDAY BOWL!*"

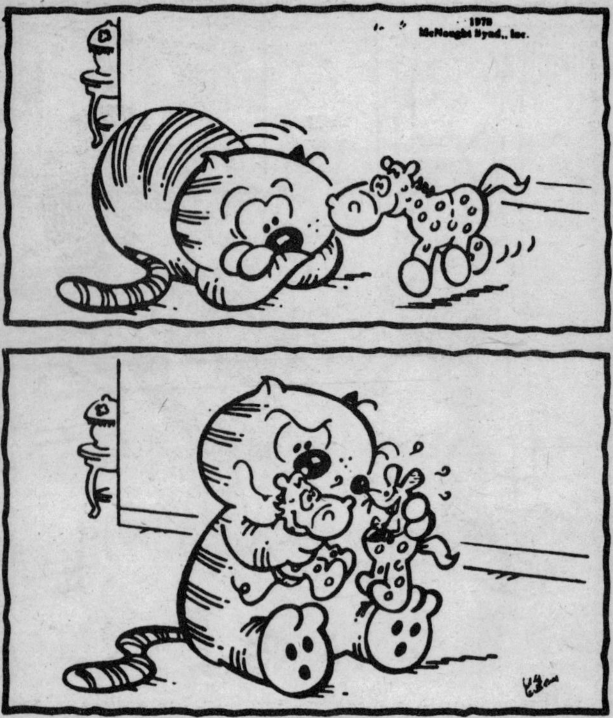
1978
McNaught Synd., Inc.

"I DON'T NEED YOUR COMPLETE HISTORY."

"I DON'T LIKE IT!"

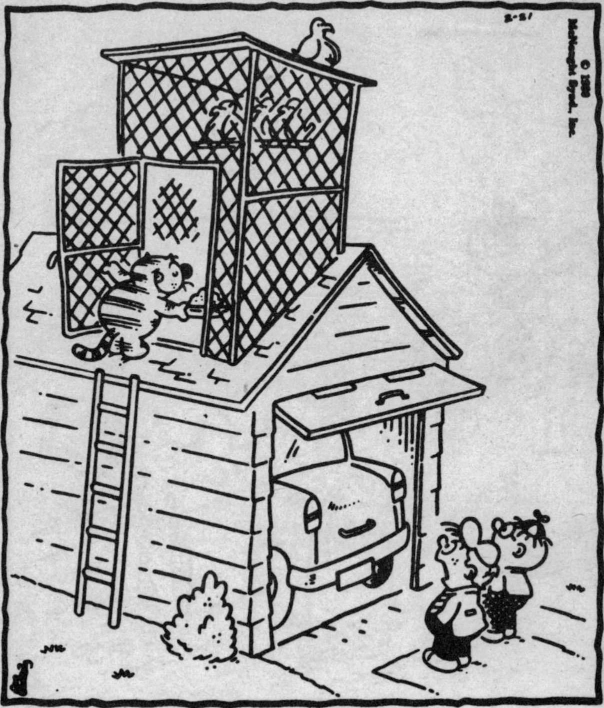

"HE'S RAISING PIGEONS!"

"THEY'RE BITING ON CUCKOOS!"

"HE DIDN'T EVEN DUMP IT!... ALL HE TOOK WAS A BANANA PEEL."

"I CAN'T FIND MY SKI MASK."

"GET OFF MY RECLINER!"

"IT'S TIME FOR TURKEY LEFTOVERS...

...SO, HE'S GOT HIMSELF A BIRD DOG!"

"BIG WEEKEND?!"

"YOU WERE SAYING...."

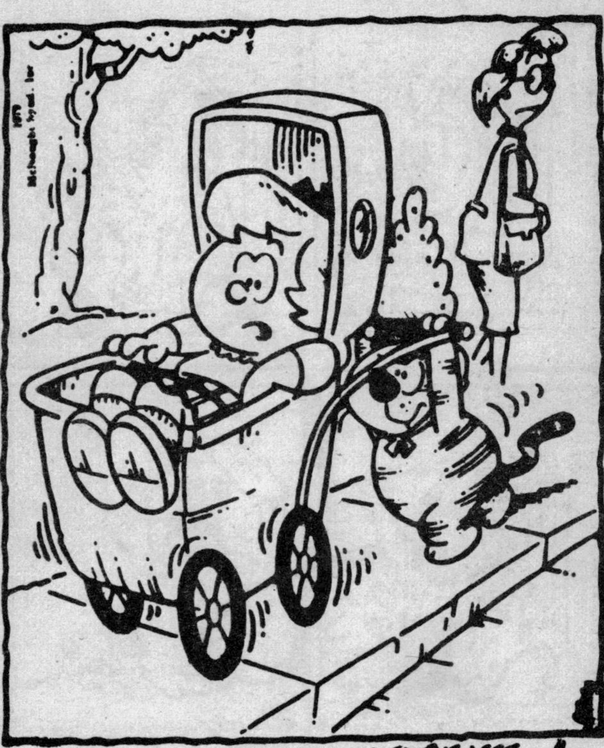

"YOU'RE RIGHT.....IT IS PULLING TO THE LEFT...."

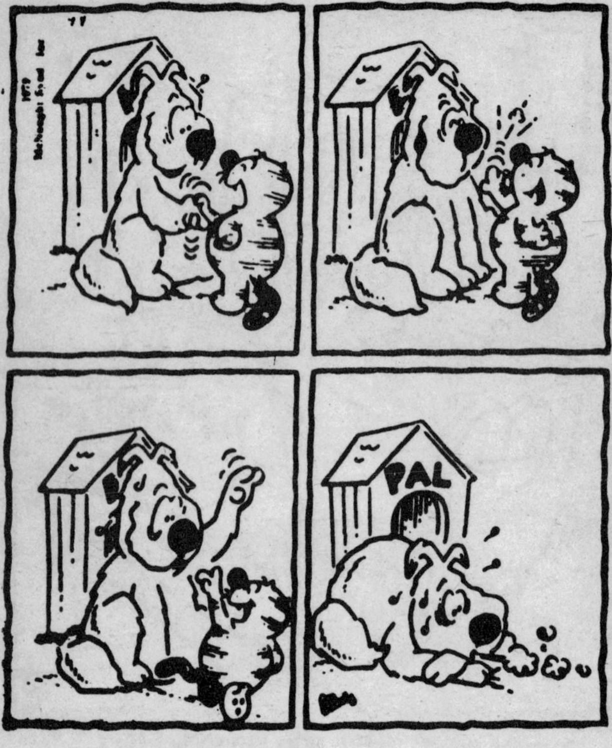
PAL

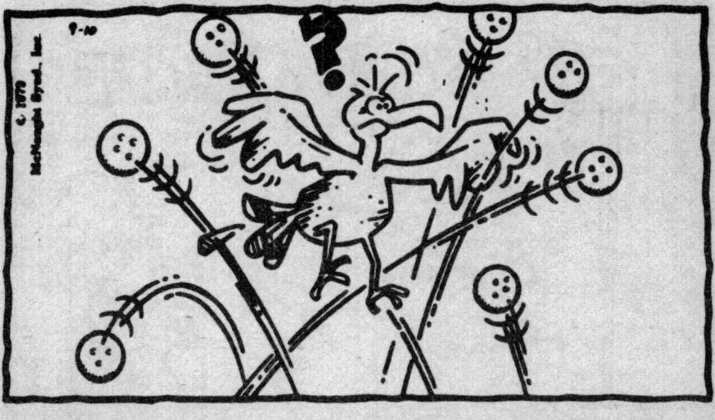
?
GOLF
DRIVING RANGE

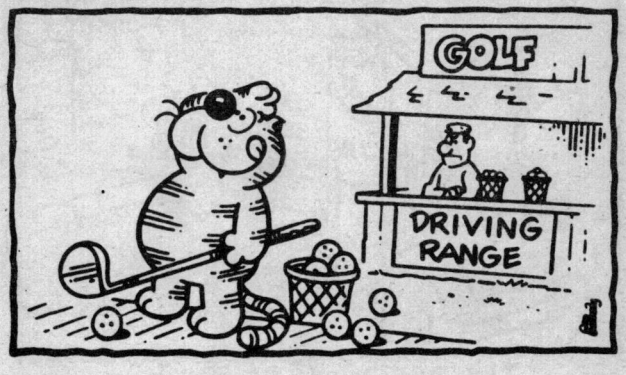

"WE JUST HANDLE THE MONEY, NOT THE CAT FOOD COUPONS."

"NOWADAYS EVERYONE WEARS BLUE JEANS... EVEN HEATHCLIFF."

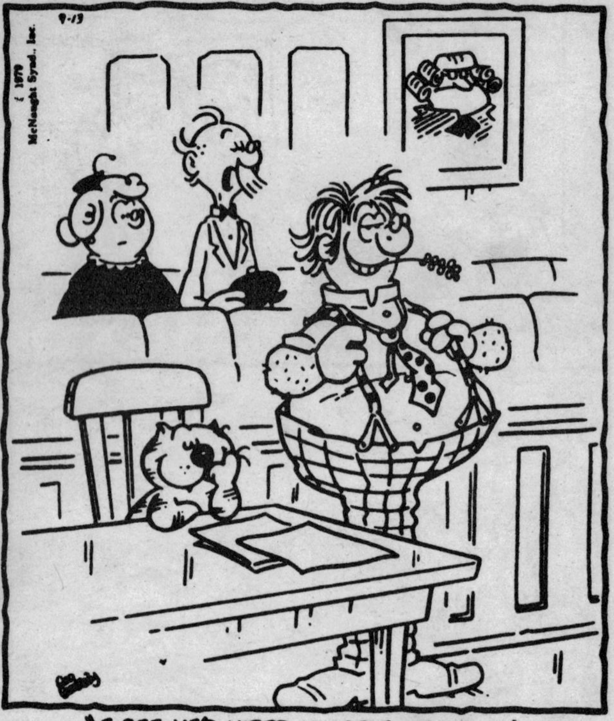

"I SEE HE'S HIRED HIMSELF A GOOD OL' DOWN HOME COUNTRY LAWYER!"

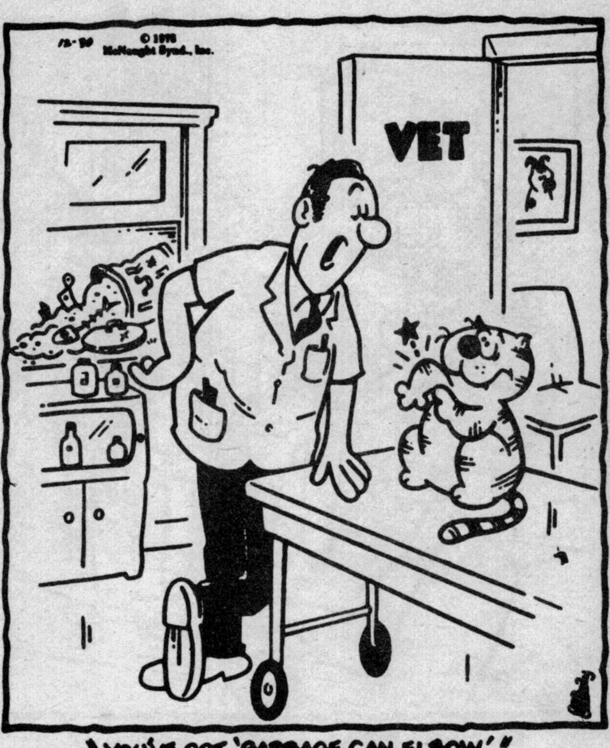

"YOU'VE GOT 'GARBAGE CAN ELBOW'."

"I'M SORRY, FRED.... I SHOULD NEVER HAVE MENTIONED THAT YOU'RE A VETERINARIAN!"

"HE'S ONE OF THE FINEST LEFTHANDERS IN THE GAME TODAY!"

"HE'S GETTING MIXED REVIEWS."

"NEEDED A LITTLE CREAM FOR YOUR COFFEE?"

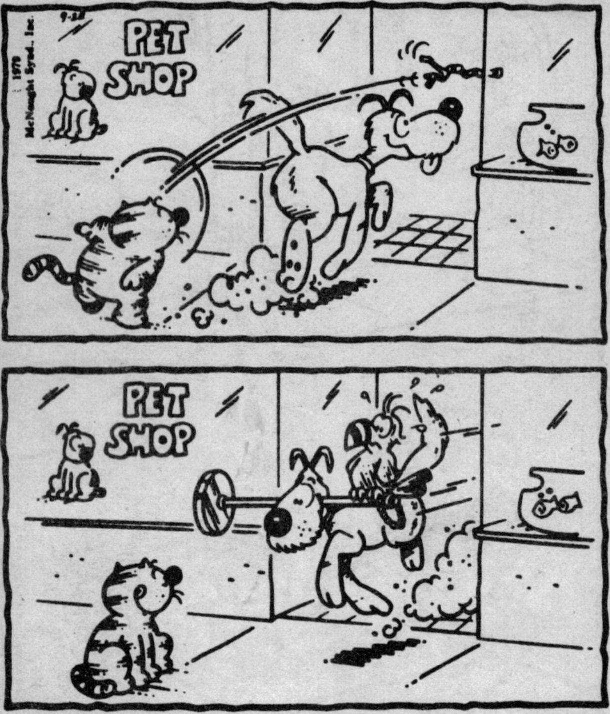
PET SHOP
1979 McNaught Synd., Inc.
PET SHOP

"DON'T LET HIM INTIMIDATE YOU."

"THAT REGISTERED A 7.4 ON THE HEATHCLIFF SCALE!"

"DOES FATSO, HERE, DO ANY TRICKS?"

"WANT YOUR WATCH?"

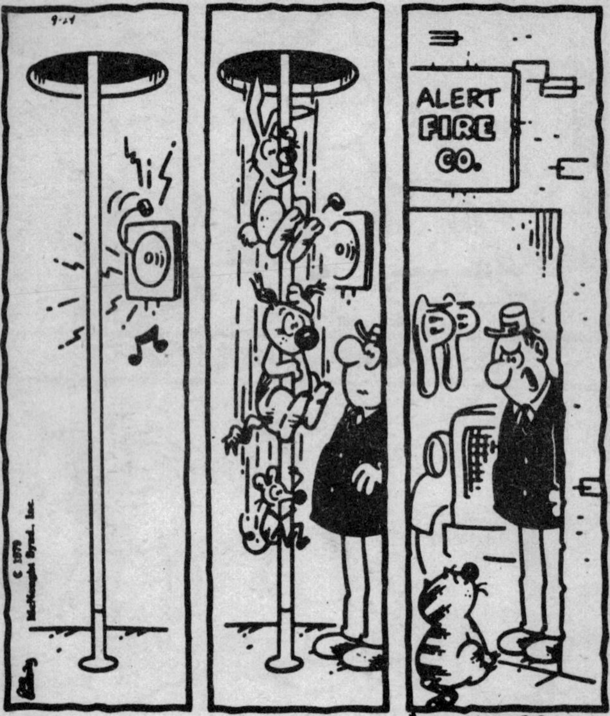

"WILL YOU STOP CHASING THOSE ANIMALS IN HERE?!"

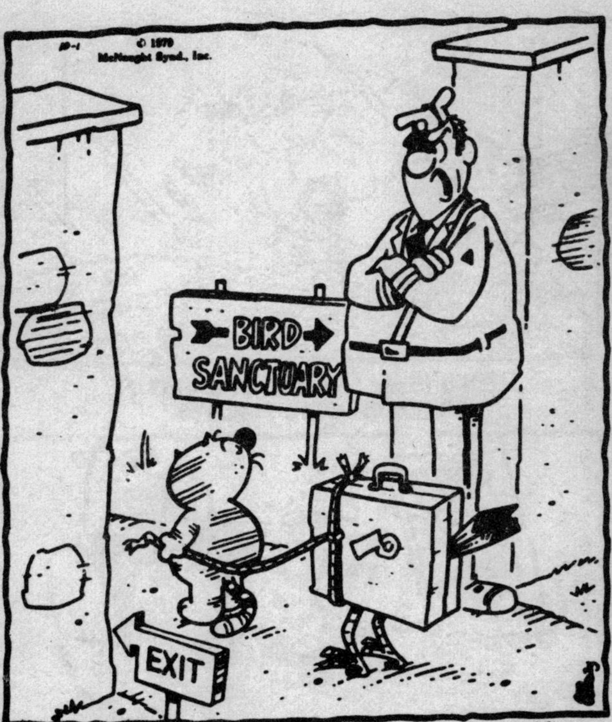

"I'LL HAVE TO EXAMINE THAT SUITCASE!"

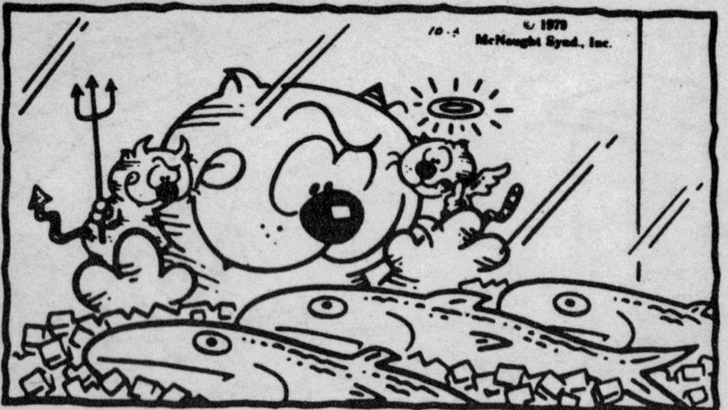

"THIS IS MY LAST PLEA, HEATHCLIFF, OR IT'S 'GOODBYE FOREVER'!"

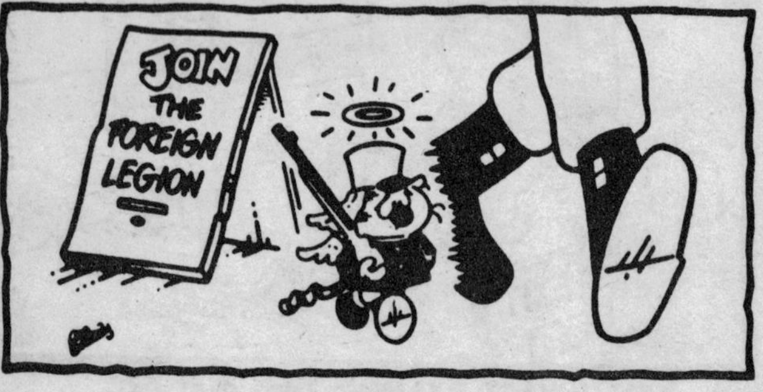

"THIS TIME I THINK HE'S SERIOUS!"

"NOT EVEN A KISS 'HELLO'?"

"HE'S VERY ACTIVE FOR HIS AGE."

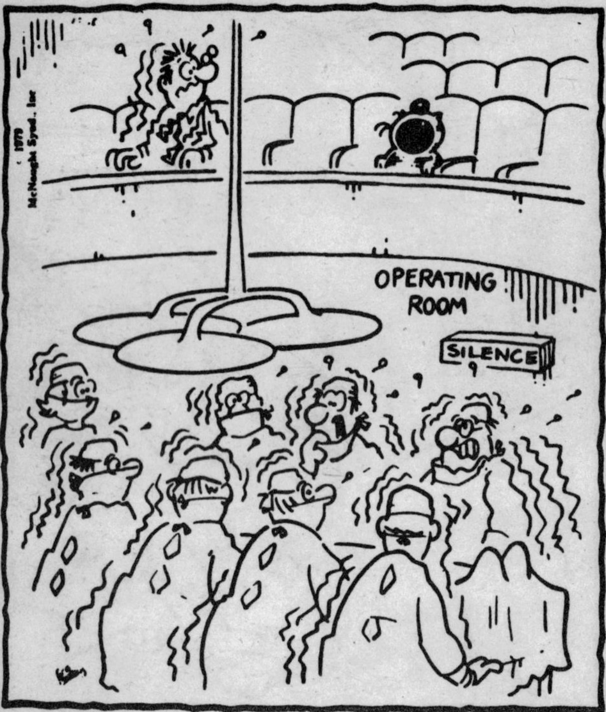

"WHAT WAS THAT BLOOD CURDLING SCREAM ALL ABOUT ?!"

"HE EATS WHERE THE TRUCK DRIVERS EAT."

"THIS IS THE LAST TIME I ORDER FISH AT A SIDEWALK CAFE!"

"CAN'T BEAT HIM AT SLAPJACK!"

"THEY STOP IN NOW AND THEN FOR A WORKOUT."

"GIFT OR NOT!... YOU CAN'T MAIL THAT!!"

"YOU REALLY GOT HIM ANGRY!"

"HERE'S A BILL FROM THE CHIROPRACTOR... 'ONE BACK SCRATCHED'!"

"I THINK IT'S A SEAFOOD RESTAURANT."

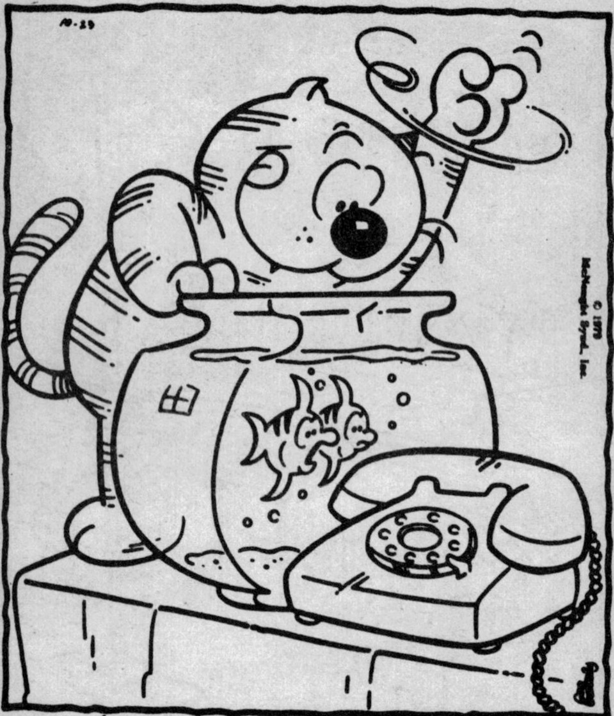

"LET'S TRY 'DIAL-A-PRAYER'!"

"WILL YOU GET HIM OUTA HERE?!"

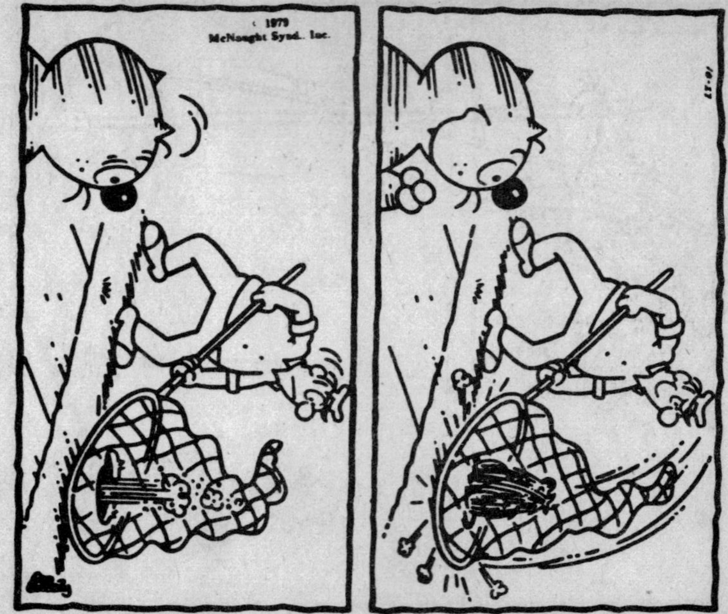
© 1979
McNaught Synd., Inc.
10-27

10-24
1979
McNaught Synd., Inc
PRIZES TO BE AWARDED
ANNUAL
CAT SHOW
JUDGE
1ST

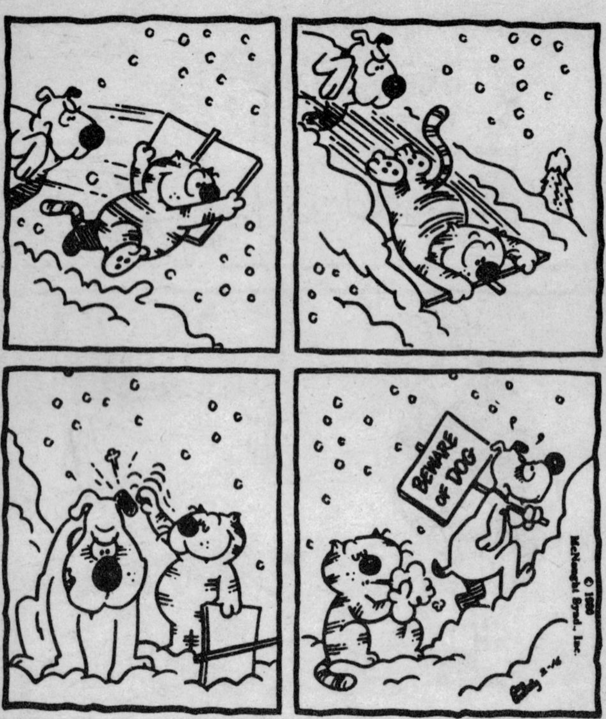
BEWARE OF DOG
McNaught Synd., Inc.

"...AND RIGHT ABOUT THERE WOULD BE THE CAT FOOD AISLE."

"WE WERE OUT FOR OUR MORNING STROLL AND HE GOT IN THIS TERRIBLE CATFIGHT!"

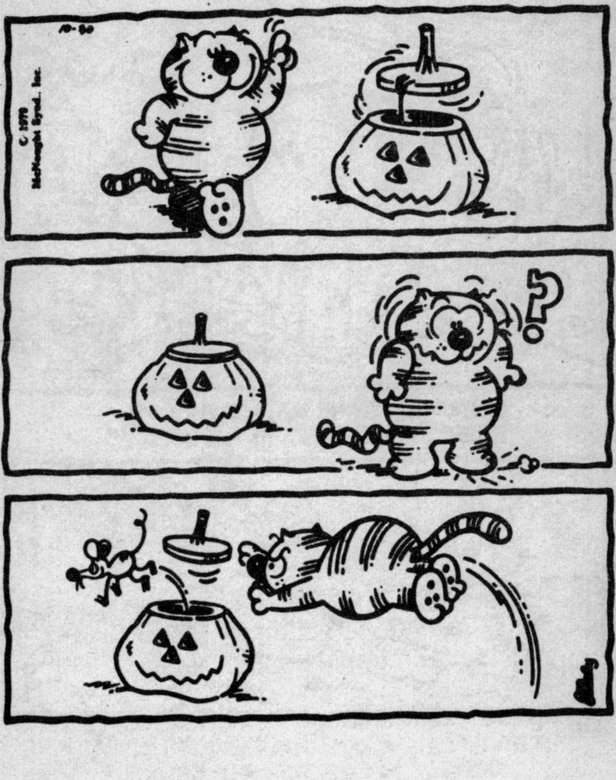

10-30
© 1979
McNaught Synd., Inc.
?!

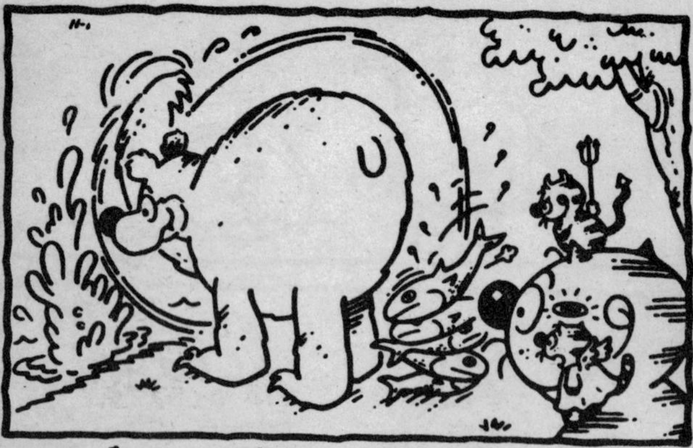

"NOW, LISTEN TO ME, HEATHCLIFF... THOSE FISH BELONG TO THE BEAR!"

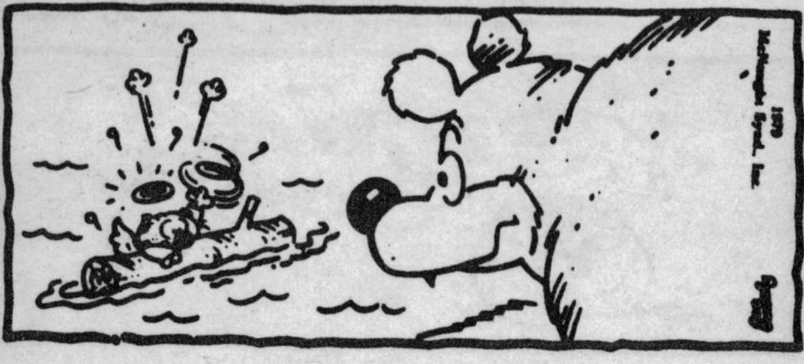

"HOW'S THE SHRIMP TODAY?"

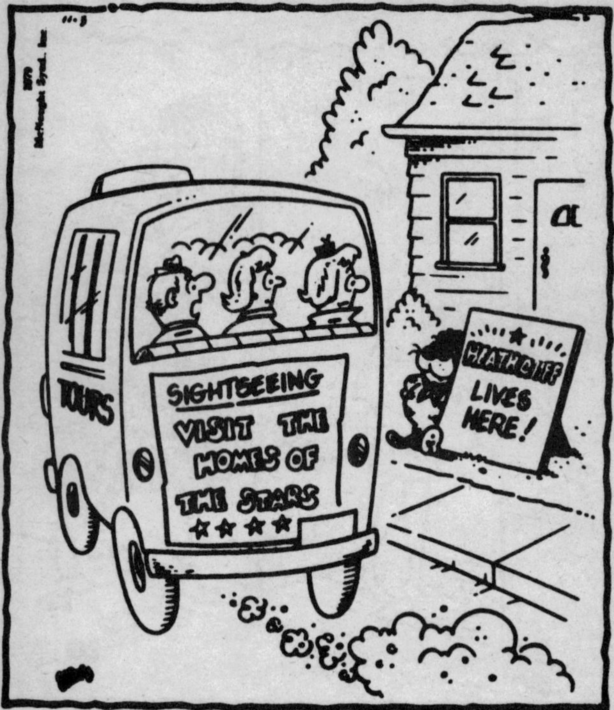

"MUST BE SOME NEW TV PERSONALITY."

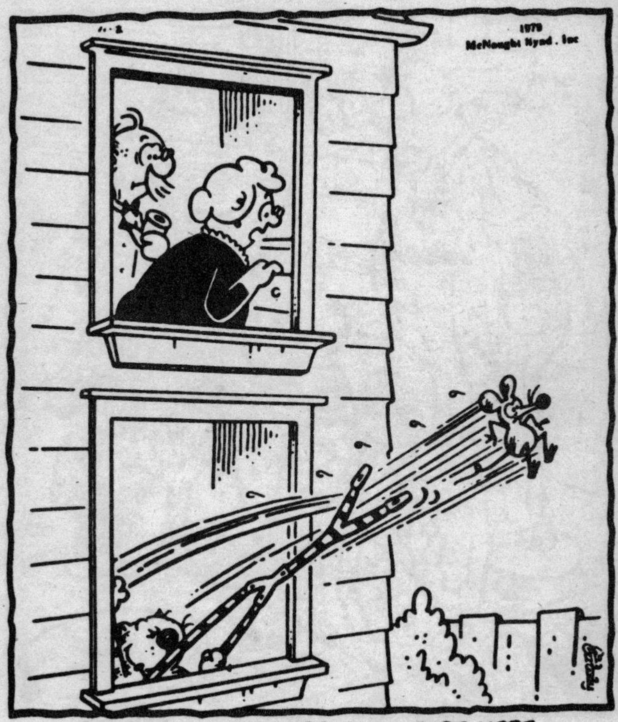

"YOUR SUSPENDERS SHOULD BE HERE
IN THIS DRAWER."

"HE'S FILLING A STOCKING FOR A HOMELESS CAT."

"NAW, I DON'T THINK A GIRL WILL EVER BE PRESIDENT... WHAT DO YOU THINK, HEATHCLIFF?"

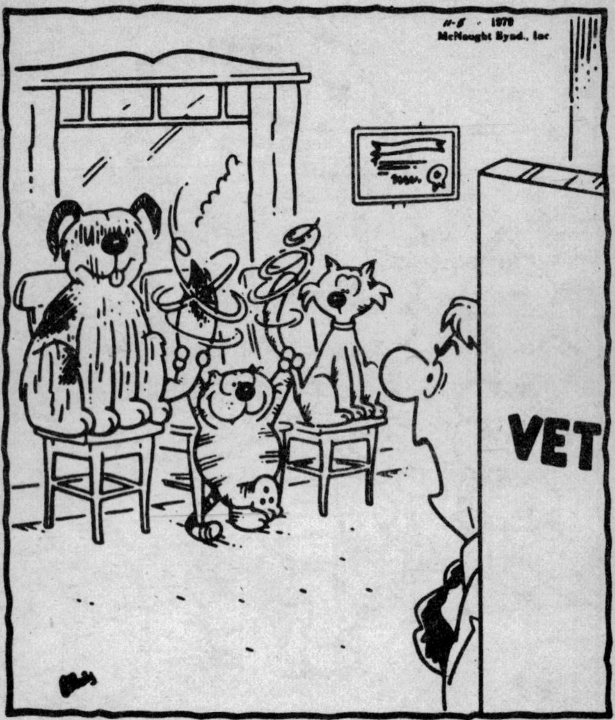

"NEXT....WAIT YOUR TURN, HEATHCLIFF!"

"AND, WOULD YOU LIKE A FOOTBATH, ALSO?!"

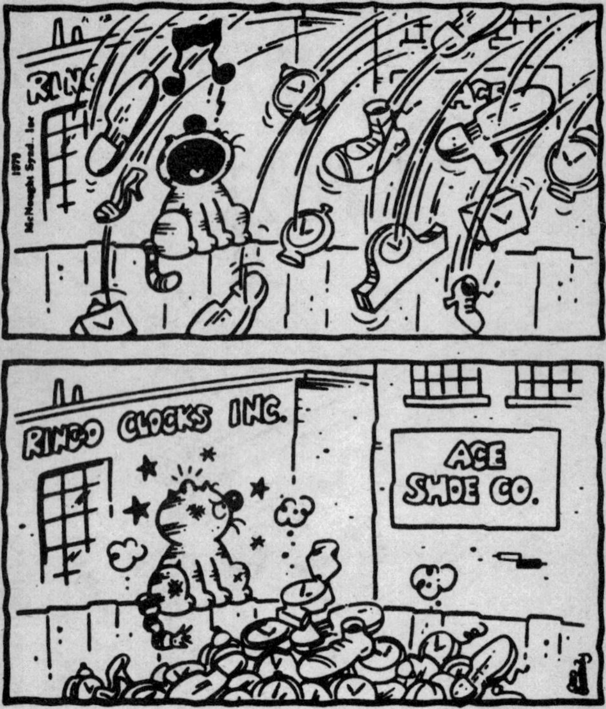

1978 McNaught Synd., Inc
RINGO CLOCKS INC.
ACE SHOE CO.

"HEATHCLIFF, YOU'RE AN INCURABLE ROMANTIC!"

"SONJA GAVE HIM A SMOKING JACKET!"

"NEXT TIME, SHE'D BETTER GIVE HIM A PIPE!"

"SOMEONE STUFFED YOUR TROMBONE INTO THE TACKLING DUMMY!"

"HE'S GOT A GIRL IN EVERY PORT!"

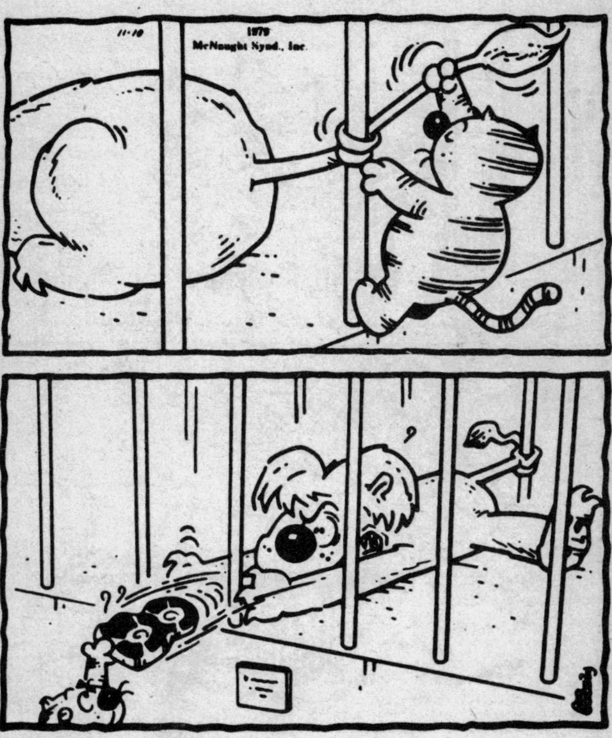
11-10
1979
McNaught Synd., Inc.

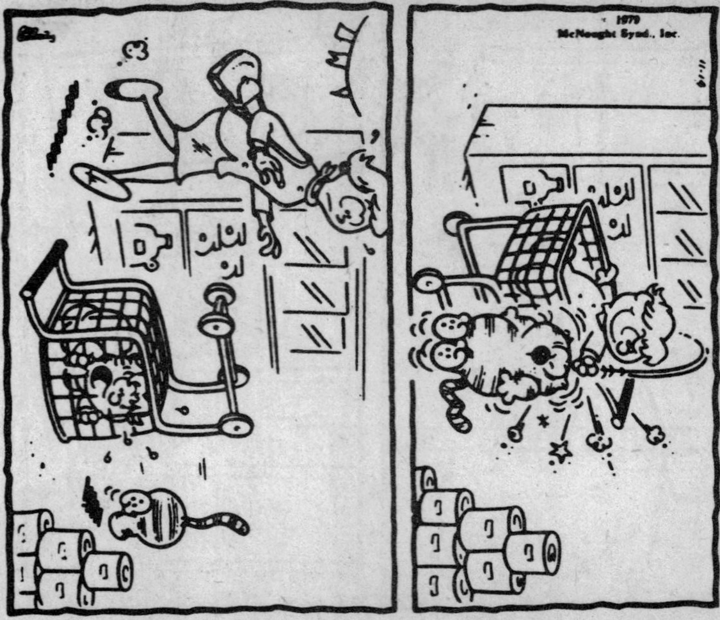

1979
McNaught Synd., Inc.

"BOO, HEATHCLIFF!"

"FORGET IT!...WE DON'T NEED IT THAT BAD!"

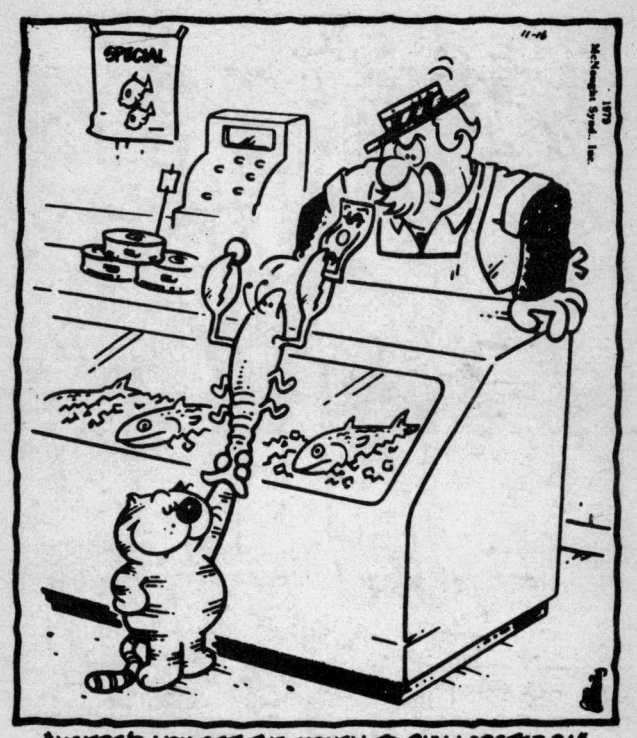

"WHERE'D YOU GET THE MONEY TO BUY LOBSTER?!"

"EEEEEEEYOWOWOW!!!"

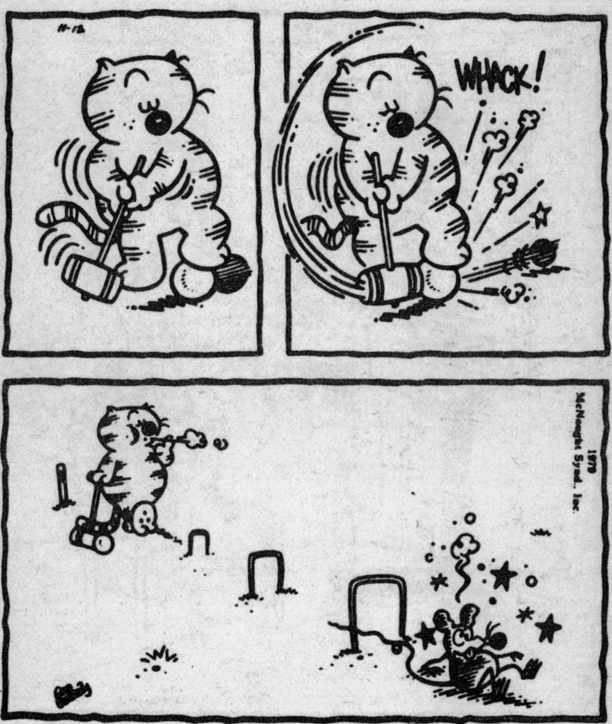
11-12
WHACK!
1979 McNaught Synd., Inc.

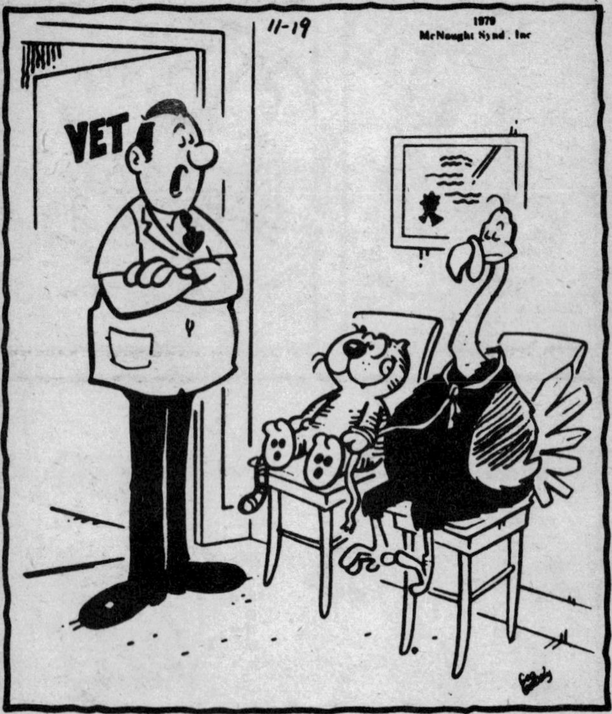

"SORRY, I DON'T DRESS TURKEYS."

"WHAT'S GOING ON HERE, FANG?!"

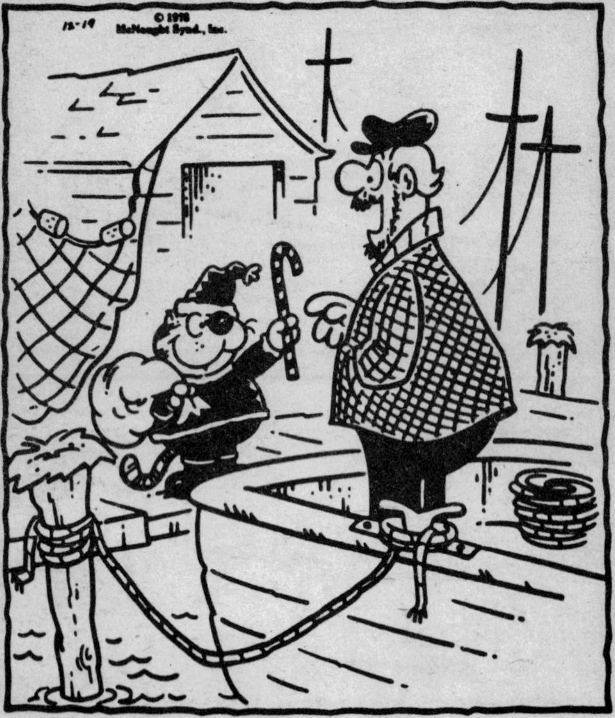

"NO ONE ELSE EVER REMEMBERS THE TUNA FLEET!"

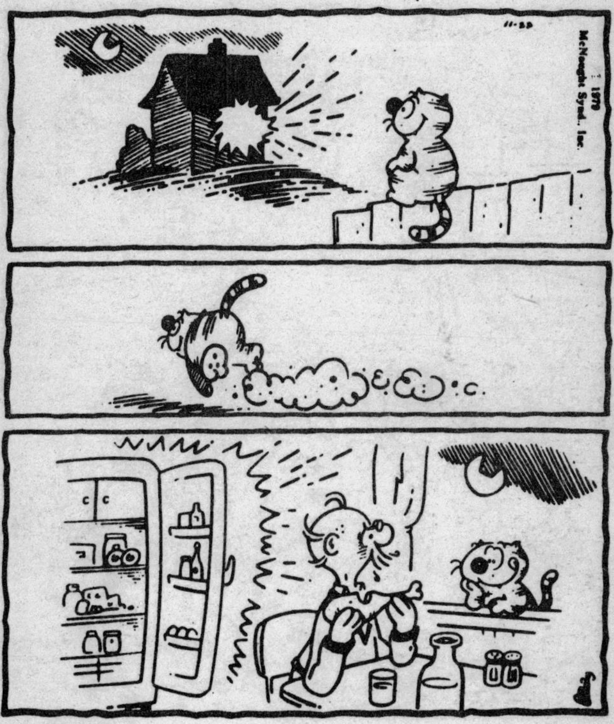
© 1979 McNaught Synd., Inc.

"NO THANKS... I'M SICK OF TURKEY SANDWICHES!"

"IT WAS THAT FAT CAT WITH THE STRIPES, AGAIN!"

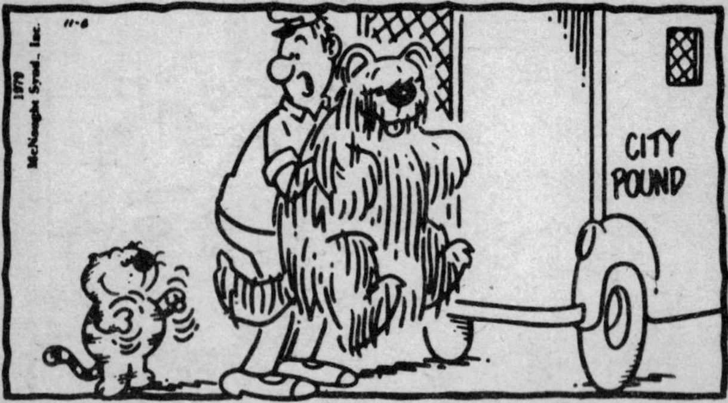

"HUH?...SHAKE HIM...??"

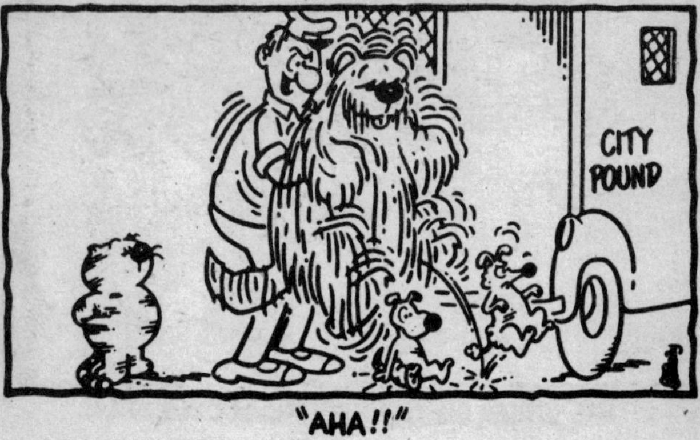

"AHA!!"

"HE'S REALLY CRACKING DOWN THIS TIME!"

"NEXT."

"I'LL TEACH HIM HIS TRICKS, THANK YOU!"

"STUFFING?...WHY WOULD I WANT TO EAT STUFFING?!"

"I'LL EDIT THE COMMERCIALS!"

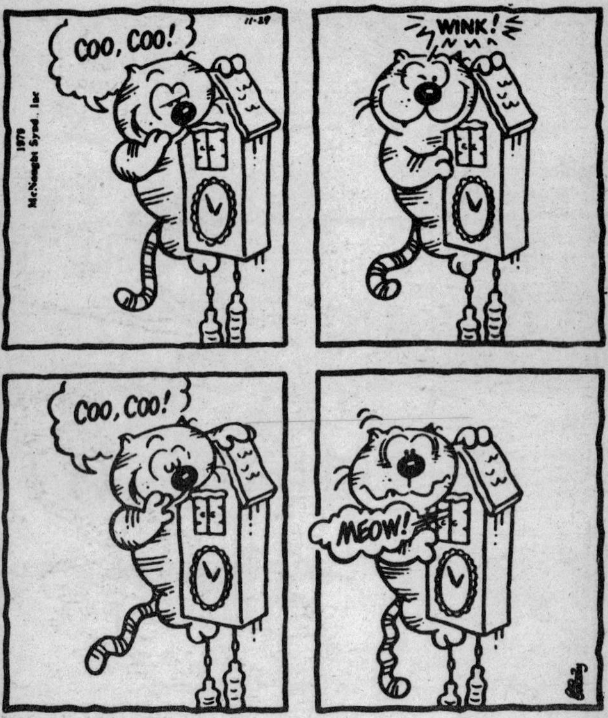
COO, COO!
WINK!
COO, COO!
MEOW!

"BEAUTIFUL TIMING, HEATHCLIFF!"

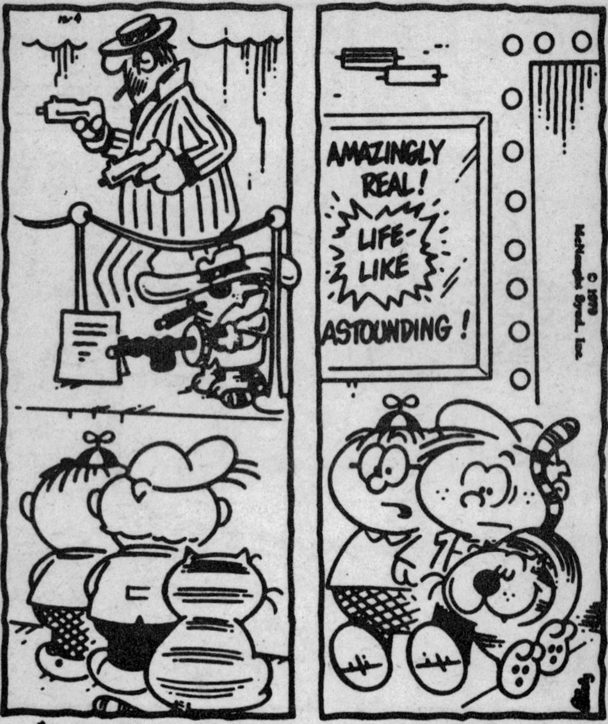

"GOLLY!...IT REALLY *IS* HEATHCLIFF!... ....IN THE WAX MUSEUM!"

"DON'T ASK!"

"THEY'RE ROASTING DOOLEY, THE DOGCATCHER."

"I THOUGHT YOU MIGHT ENJOY SOME CRACKERS AND CATNIP DIP."

"SOUP'S ON!"

"IF YOU'RE THIRSTY, THIS WILL HAVE TO DO.... WE'RE FRESH OUT OF BOTTLED SPRING WATER!"

"DINNERTIME, HEATHCLIFF....

...AND TAKE IT EASY....I JUST WAXED THE FLOOR!"

"I THINK THE OLD FOOL HAS GONE CRACKERS!"

"IT'S ONLY A MATTER OF TIME BEFORE THE RAILROAD COMES THROUGH HERE!"